Sweet Pea & Friends

The Easter Surprise

By John and Jennifer Churchman

LB

LITTLE, BROWN AND COMPANY
NEW YORK   BOSTON

Fern woke up to a warm spring breeze tickling her nose. *It's morning!* she thought excitedly. Sweet Pea the sheep had promised her a surprise today. Fern hopped toward the barn to find out what it could be.

As she passed the old maple tree, Fern heard two squirrels *chit-chitter*ing to each other. "I didn't put it there. Did you put it there? No, *I* didn't put it there. Did *you* put it there?"

Put what where? Fern wondered. She looked up and saw a beautifully decorated egg. *How pretty. The picture on that egg looks just like Mo the farm kitten.* Fern decided to ask him about it before going to find Sweet Pea.

Fern discovered Mo prowling around the kitchen garden. "Look what I found," Mo said, pointing to the colorful eggs hiding among the lettuce. "This one has a picture on it that reminds me of Keeper the goose."

"This feels like a *mystery*!" exclaimed Fern. She loved following clues. "Come on, let's go find Keeper!"

Fern and Mo hurried to the pond, where Keeper was watching over her baby goslings. All three were honking excitedly. "We found fancy eggs!" said Rose from on top of her mother's back. "This one has a picture of a puppy on it," peeped Myrtle.

"The next clue! Everyone, follow me," said Fern. But Mo was busy batting at a dragonfly headed back to its home in the wildflower field. "Mo, come on!"

The friends ran to the orchard, where they heard the sheepdog puppies yipping and yapping as they chased several brightly colored eggs down the hill. "Do you know who is leaving these eggs around the farm?" Tosh asked Fern. "This one has a picture of ducklings on it!"

"No, it's a mystery," said Fern. "We'll stop to see Sweet Pea on the way to the ducklings. Maybe she'll know what's going on."

Just then, a rustle made Fern look behind her. Were those soft, pointy ears peeking out above the grass? She blinked, and the ears were gone. *That's curious*, she thought.

When the friends reached the barn, the sheep were *baa-baa*ing to one another. Little Finn had found a colorful egg in his hay! "It has a picture of a rooster on it," said Violet.

"First ducklings and now a rooster. We're
definitely going to the chicken house next,"
said Fern. "But wait—is Sweet Pea here?"

"No, we haven't seen her all morning,"
said Little Finn.

No one had seen Sweet Pea at the chicken house, either, but the chicks, turkey poults, and ducklings joined in the egg hunt. They searched here and there, up and down, running all around. "We can't find any fancy eggs!" they cried in dismay.

How can we solve the mystery without a clue to follow? thought Fern.

"Squawk!" All of a sudden, Mother Hen lifted her large feathery body off her nest. Decorated eggs were piled high *underneath* her! And right on top was one with a picture of Lilly the lamb.

Something else caught Fern's eye. It looked like a big fluffy tail disappearing behind the barn. "Did you see that?" she asked Mo.

"See what?" he asked, rolling an egg in front of him. "Come on, let's go find Lilly!"

The friends met Lilly and the other lambs in the spring pasture. "We've been finding eggs all over the field," said Lilly.

Just then Scout peeked out from
behind a lilac bush. "I found another
one!" It was a bright green egg with
a picture of a big ram on it.

Everyone got very quiet. "Uh-oh…"
said Fern.

The friends lined up along the ram pen. They could see a pretty egg inside but couldn't reach it. Tweed the grumpy ram snorted and stomped his hoof.

"Let's find Maisie and Laddie," suggested Fern. "They'll know how to get that egg." But as she turned to lead everyone away, she saw long whiskers twitching in the flowers. *Could it be Sweet Pea? No, Sweet Pea doesn't have whiskers.*

Maisie and Laddie the sheepdogs were with
Sadie the pony. There was a decorated egg
balancing on Sadie's fence.

"An egg has rolled into grumpy
Tweed's pen!" Fern exclaimed.
"Can you help us get it out?"

Laddie and Maisie quickly followed her back to the pen. Everyone sat perfectly still while Maisie distracted Tweed, and Laddie gently pulled the pretty egg to safety with his paw. On it was the next clue—a picture of Poppy the alpaca! "She'll be in the meadow!" said Fern.

The alpacas were having their late-afternoon snack when Fern and her friends arrived. "There's a topsy-turvy row of eggs tucked in our grass," said Poppy. "We even found one with a picture of Sweet Pea on it."

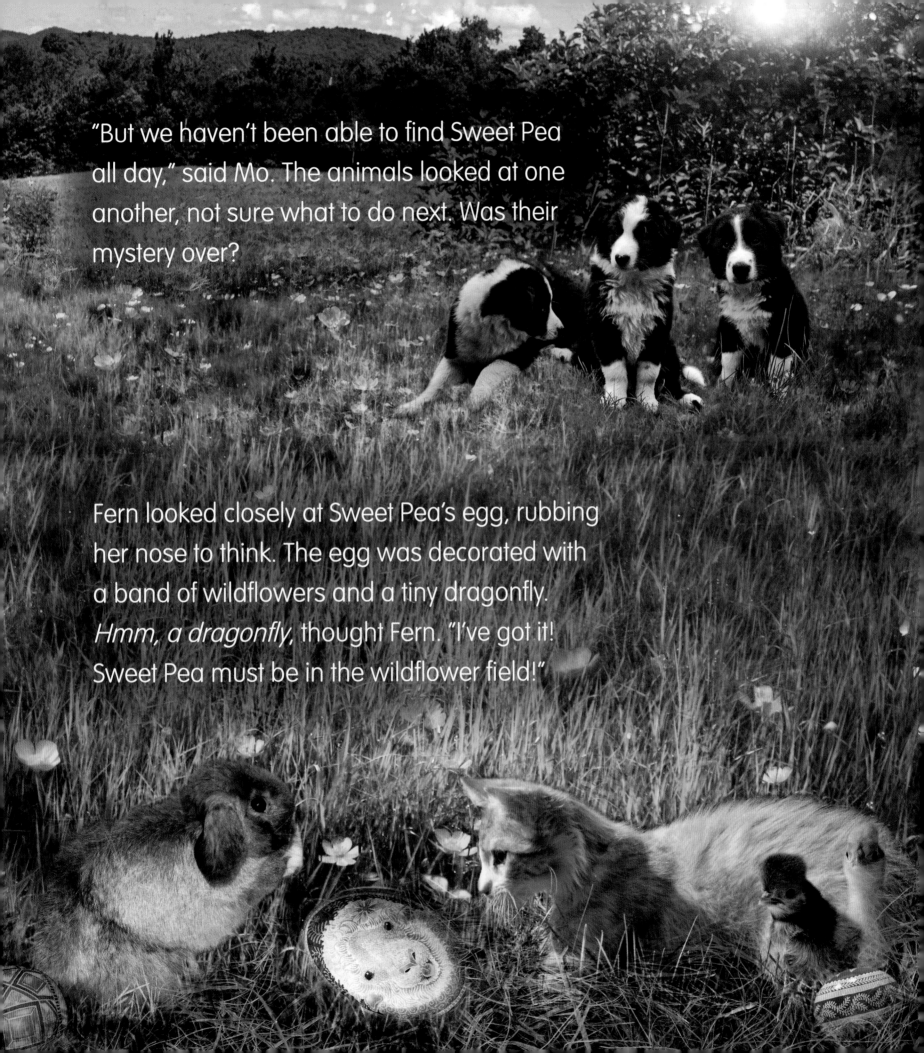

"But we haven't been able to find Sweet Pea all day," said Mo. The animals looked at one another, not sure what to do next. Was their mystery over?

Fern looked closely at Sweet Pea's egg, rubbing her nose to think. The egg was decorated with a band of wildflowers and a tiny dragonfly. *Hmm, a dragonfly,* thought Fern. "I've got it! Sweet Pea must be in the wildflower field!"

"Follow me!" said Fern.

It was getting dark when at last Fern saw Sweet Pea at the far end of the wildflower field. She was talking to the biggest bunny Fern had ever seen!

By the time the friends reached Sweet Pea, the bunny had disappeared. But a large basket of beautiful eggs sat in the grass, and right on top was the fanciest egg of all. "That's me!" said Fern.

"Yes," said Sweet Pea. "You solved the mystery. And you've just been on your first Easter egg hunt!"

Fern bounced happily. It *had* been a mystery— and she had solved it with the help of her friends.

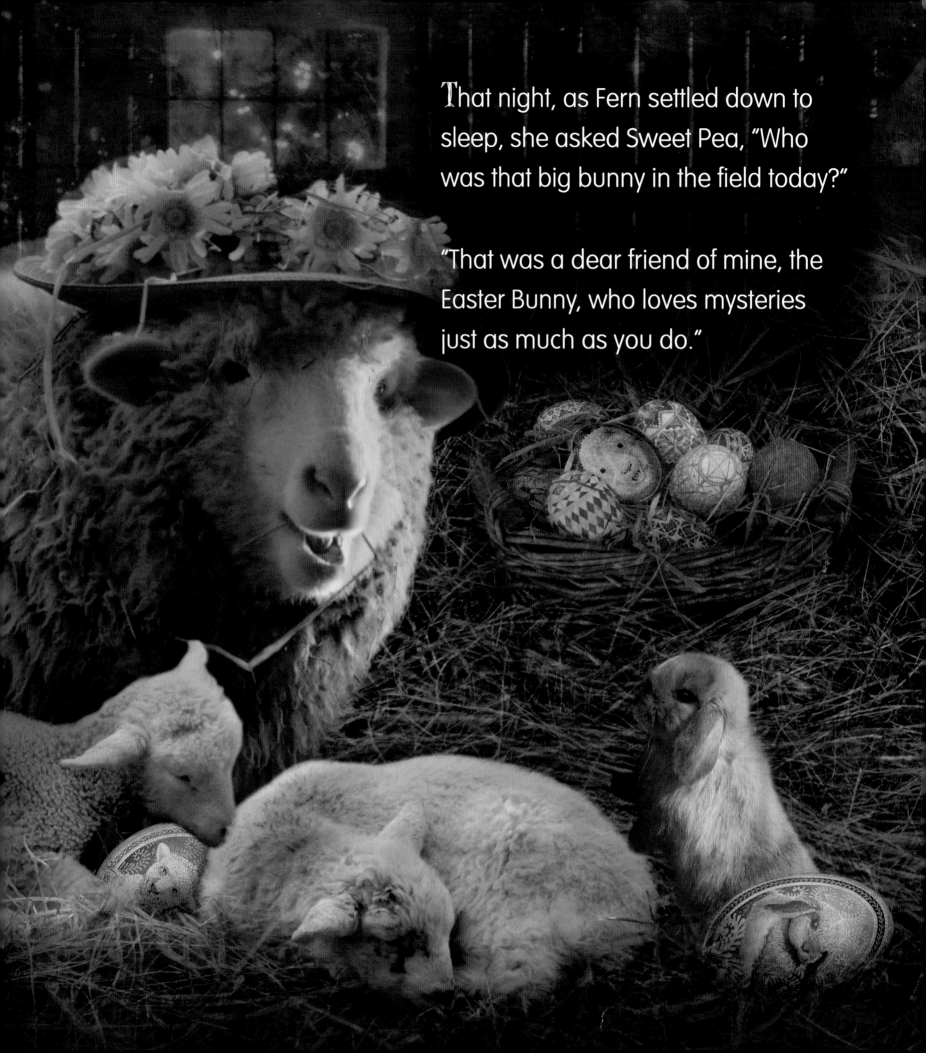

That night, as Fern settled down to sleep, she asked Sweet Pea, "Who was that big bunny in the field today?"

"That was a dear friend of mine, the Easter Bunny, who loves mysteries just as much as you do."

Fern yawned. "Thank you for such a special surprise."

"You're welcome," whispered Sweet Pea.
"Happy Easter, Fern, and good night."

The True Story of Fern

At the time of writing this story, Fern was a very young bunny—about six months old and tiny enough to hold in one hand! She is a Holland Lop, the smallest of the lop-eared rabbits, with ears that "helicopter out" when she's surprised. (Lop-eared rabbits have ears that hang down instead of stick up.) Fern enjoys bouncing around the garden, investigating crevices in the stone wall, and peering under every vegetable leaf. Mo the kitten came to Moonrise Farm about the same time that Fern did, and everywhere Fern went, Mo would follow close behind, making paths in the flower fields and the garden together. We wanted their friendship in real life to be a part of Fern's story in this book.

Who Is That Easter Bunny? It's *Willow*!

Willow is a Flemish Giant rabbit that we adopted along with her sister Flossie from the Chittenden County Humane Society. Flemish Giants are the largest rabbit breed and can weigh more than fifteen pounds and grow up to two and a half feet long! They are friendly, gentle, and curious, and they love digging tunnels. Willow particularly loves hiding toys and carrots in the straw-filled play area of the barn and finding them again with Flossie. Willow is such an expert at hiding things (including herself!) that we thought she would make the perfect Easter Bunny.

An Easter Seek-and-Find

Sweet Pea's dear friend the Easter Bunny is on almost every page of this story! Sometimes Fern even catches a glimpse. Can you find pointy bunny ears, twitching whiskers, and bouncing paws hiding throughout the book? Do you see a fluffy round tail peeking out from behind the barn? Sometimes the Easter Bunny might even be disguised as a bunch of flowers, so make sure you look closely. Then count the Easter eggs throughout the book. How many can you find? Turn the page to see the answer.

Collaboration with Theresa Somerset, Ukrainian Egg Artist

Our talented friend Theresa Somerset has been using our farm-fresh eggs for her beautiful Ukrainian egg art for years. She especially likes to use the light green duck eggs, the tiny pullet eggs (eggs from a chicken that is less than one year old), the huge white goose eggs, and the rare blue eggs from Whiting True Blue chickens as the canvases for her amazing creations. She worked closely with us during the creation of *The Easter Surprise* to create the beautiful batik-style "clue eggs" with animal portraits found throughout the book. The other eggs used in the book are a mix of batik and traditional and nontraditional Ukrainian *pysanka* art styles from her personal egg art collection.

Theresa has been a studio artist for thirty years and has practiced the art of batik eggs for the last eighteen years. She teaches, lectures, and displays her work around the world and is a member of the prestigious International Egg Art Guild and World Egg Artists Associated. You can enjoy more of Theresa's work at www.precisionartstudio.com.

Dedicated with love to our children, Kailie, Travis, and Gabrielle, and to Jennifer's sister Gillian and brother Michael for the many wonderful Easter egg–hunting memories at their childhood home, Stillmeadow Farm

Little, Brown and Company
Hachette Book Group
1290 Avenue of the Americas, New York, NY 10104
Visit us at LBYR.com

First Edition: February 2019

Little, Brown and Company is a division of Hachette Book Group, Inc.
The Little, Brown name and logo are trademarks of Hachette Book Group, Inc.

The publisher is not responsible for websites (or their content) that are not owned by the publisher.

Library of Congress Cataloging-in-Publication Data
Names: Churchman, John, 1957– author, illustrator. | Churchman, Jennifer, author.
Title: The Easter surprise / by John and Jennifer Churchman.
Description: First edition. | New York ; Boston : Little, Brown and Company, 2019. | Series: Sweet Pea & friends ; 5 |
Summary: "Curious bunny Fern is determined to find all the beautifully decorated eggs on the farm in a springtime mystery." —Provided by publisher.
Identifiers: LCCN 2018009913| ISBN 9780316411660 (hardcover) | ISBN 9780316411677 (ebook) | ISBN 9780316411707 (library edition ebook)
Subjects: | CYAC: Easter eggs—Fiction. | Easter egg hunts—Fiction. | Rabbits—Fiction. | Domestic animals—Fiction. | Animals—Infancy—Fiction. | Mystery and detective stories.
Classification: LCC PZ7.1.C55 Eas 2019 | DDC [E]—dc23
LC record available at https://lccn.loc.gov/2018009913

ISBNs: 978-0-316-41166-0 (hardcover)
978-0-316-41167-7 (ebook)
978-0-316-41169-1 (ebook)
978-0-316-41168-4 (ebook)

Printed in China

1010

10 9 8 7 6 5 4 3 2 1

There are 120 Easter eggs in this book.